T0114560

LOVE AT TENTH SIGHT

A SHORT NOVEL OF
LOVE AND MURDER

DON LIGHT

authorHOUSE®

AuthorHouse™
1663 Liberty Drive
Bloomington, IN 47403
www.authorhouse.com
Phone: 1 (800) 839-8640

Published by AuthorHouse 07/19/2016

ISBN: 978-1-5246-1907-7 (sc)
ISBN: 978-1-5246-1906-0 (e)

Print information available on the last page.

Any people depicted in stock imagery provided by Thinkstock are models,
and such images are being used for illustrative purposes only.
Certain stock imagery © Thinkstock.

This book is printed on acid-free paper.

Because of the dynamic nature of the Internet, any web addresses or links contained in
this book may have changed since publication and may no longer be valid. The views
expressed in this work are solely those of the author and do not necessarily reflect the
views of the publisher, and the publisher hereby disclaims any responsibility for them.

This is a work of fiction. The city of Bloomington, Indiana, where most of the action takes place, is real, as is Indiana University. The resemblence of any character to any person, living or dead, is purely coincidental.

To Rita, Naomi, and Rebecca

Chapter 1

In mid morning David Stein entered a convenience store to buy a paperback. He saw a young girl at the counter buying some toiletries, but there were no other customers in the place.

David's first thought about the the girl was that she was beautiful: five feet six inches tall, about twenty-one years old, slim waist and excellent figure. He could not take his eyes off her. David himself was tall, about six feet two inches, slim, and twenty-five.

The store was located in Bloomington, Indiana, on Kirkwood Avenue, just west of the campus of Indiana University. It was late March, after the students had returned from spring break.

Suddenly a shot rang out and the man collecting cash from the girl mumbled, "Oh," and crumpled to the floor. David rushed to him, but saw a bullet hole in his forehead and guessed that he was dead. He then turned around but did not see anyone with a gun either inside or outside the store.

He looked at his watch: it was 10:05 a.m., March 23. Then he called 911 on his cell phone to give the details and to get the police and an amublance as soon as possible.

The girl seemed to be in shock at first but recovered and knelt down beside the fallen clerk.

"I think he's dead," she said to David.

"I thought so too and called the police," he answered. "We'll both have to stay here to answer questions."

"I'm in a hurry. I have to get to class."

"You'll have to skip your class today. There's a dead man here, and you're a witness."

"But I didn't see who shot him," said the girl. "I can have nothing to add to what you saw."

"Nevertheless, you saw him shot. You saw the time. Maybe there's something else you can add, but whether you can or can't, you'll have to stay until the police arrive."

"I didn't think to look at the time," said the girl.

"My nane is Dave. What's yours?"

"None of your business," she said.

"You'll have to tell it to the police, and I'll hear it," he replied, not being able to repress a smile.

Just then, siren blaring, a police car pulled over outside the store. Twe uniformed men quickly entered.

"What's going on here?" said one.

David answered, "This girl and I were shopping here when we heard a shot. The clerk fell down with a bullet hole in his forehead. The time was 10:05. By the time I turned around to look who shot him, the killer was gone."

"It's probably a good thing," said the officer. "If you had seen the killer, you might have been shot too."

The officer fell to his knees beside the man lying down. "He's dead all right. And what can you tell me?" he asked the girl.

"Nothing except that I knelt down beside him and felt for a pulse. He didn't have one. I didn't look at my watch. When I looked around, the person who shot him was gone."

"What are your names?" asked the policeman.

"David Stein."

"Ruth Anders."

Another car arrived, and a man and woman in civilian clothes entered.

"We're detectives," said the man, showing a badge. "We hear there's a dead man around, Where is he?"

One of the uniformed officers said, "Behind this counter. He was shot right between the eyes. He's dead for sure."

With a wailing siren, an ambulance arrived. Two men entered.

"Where's the man who was shot?" asked one.

"Behind this counter. He's dead."

The men from the ambulance rushed to the fallen man. "He's dead all right," said one after putting his ear to the man's chest.

"You can't do anything for him now," said the plain-clothes officer. Leave him there until we get a team to take photos and examine the body. They'll be here soon."

The woman plainclothes officer asked, "Were this man and woman witnesses? Let's hear what they have to say."

David and Ruth repeated what they had already said.

"Is that all?" said the woman detective. "you don't have any idea who shot him?"

"We didn't see the person with the gun. we don't even know whether the killer was a man or a woman," said David.

"My name is Bruce Ritter, and the lady is Marge Wiley. We're both with the Bloomington police. And now let's hear some more from both of you."

They took down statements from David and Ruth with names, home and email addresses, and phone numbers.

"What are your occupations?" asked Ritter.

"I'm an undergrad studying biology." said Ruth.

"And I'm a grad student in math," said David.

Ritter said to David, "I'm going to have to search you to see whether you have a gun or anything else incriminating. Marge will search Ruth in another room."

"I have no objection," said David.

"Nor have I," added Ruth.

The inspections were carried out swiftly and yielded nothing of interest.

"You're both clean. If you had a gun, you hid it somewhere. We'll search the store for it. You're free to go now, but we may call you back at any time," said the plainclothes detective. "So don't go out of town without informing us."

"My number is a cell. I don't have a landline," said Ruth.

"Just write that down beside the number," said the detective.

David wrote down both his landline and cell numbers, marking them appropriately.

Then they both left the store.

Ritter and Wiley both went to investigate neighboring stores on either side of the one in which Jim Mercer was killed. They spoke to the people behind the counters, but nobody knew anything. One woman heard what might have been a shot, but which at the time she thought was a backfire.

She did not look at her watch.

"Nothing to go on here," said Ritter to Wiley. "Our only leads are the man and woman who were in the store when we arrived."

"I don't think they did it," said Wiley. If they did, they would have just walked away and not called the police."

"You may be right," Ritter replied, "but I'm not sure. We'll have to follow up. Who knows what they were thinking? And besides, we have no other suspects."

"Maybe if we question people Mercer knew, we'll find suspects."

"It's a wild goose chase," said Ritter. "I say we concentrate on the suspects we have."

Once outside the store, Ruth said, "I've never before been in a place and saw somebody murdered. To tell you the truth, I'm shocked. I've never witnessed a murder anywhere."

"Well, you have now."

"It's a frightening experience."

"The poor guy who got shot had no time to be frightened."

"I guess that's a good thing, if anything about this is a good thing."

"Well," said David, "So long. See you around."

"Will you?"

"As long as this case goes unsolved, I'm sure of it."

"Maybe the police will solve it quickly," said Ruth.

"I hope you're right," said David, "but I doubt it. Where are the clues?"

They parted, David walking one way and Ruth another.

Chapter 2

The next day David and Ruth were called to the police station. David walked. It was chilly and cloudy. "It might rain," he thought.

The rain held off. When he arreived, Ruth was already there. They were ushered into a small roomm, which was empty except for a table with a pad of paper and pens, four chairs, and a lamp. They were greeted by the plainclothes detectives.

"Hi. I'm sure you remember Marge and me from yesterday."

"Of course, Mr. Ritter."

"Call me Bruce, and I'll call you Dave. All right?"

"That will be fine, Bruce."

"And I'll call you Ruth," Ritter said to the girl. "Now Dave and Ruth, both of you sit down, if you don't mind."

They sat down. The detectives remained standing.

"Now please tell your stories of just what happened yesterday," said Ritter.

"But we already told you," said Ruth.

"Tell us again."

"They want to test us for consistency," David whispered

to Ruth.

"Please, just tell us what happened. No side comments," said Ritter.

They repeated their stories, Ruth first, and then David. There were no essential differences from those of the previous day.

Ritter then asked, "Do you two know each other?"

"Now we do," said Ruth. "We didn't before the shooting."

Wiley said, "Unfortunately, we have absolutely no confirmation of your statements of yesterday and today."

"No one else was there. How could you get confirmation?" asked Ruth.

"We don't even know if somebody else inside or outside the store shot Jim Mercer."

"So that was his name," said Ruth without thinking.

"If you don't mind, just answer the questions that are asked."

"OK," said David.

"Sorry," said Ruth. "It won't happen again."

"Now as I was saying," repeated Wiley. "We don't know anything about somebody shooting Mercer from outside. We don't know there *was* anybody outside. We have to investigate the possibility that one of you shot him."

"Absolutely not," said David. "If we had, would we have called the police and waited for them in the store? Besides, where is the gun?"

"You tell *me*," said Ritter.

"What you are saying doesn't make any sense to me," said David. "If we had killed Mr. Mercer, we wouldn't have called 911 and hung around until the police arrived."

"What you're saying doesn't make sense," echoed Ruth. "There would be no reason for us to call the police and then wait arund for them if we had killed Mercer."

"Please, no comments on whether we make sense or not."

"Sorry," Ruth repeated.

"But to answer your question, somebody may have seen you in the store."

"Except for the killer and us, anybody else here was a mythical person," said David, "not counting Mercer."

"Don't get sarcastic with me," snarled Ritter, "or we'll take you in for obstructing justice. The fact is that we only have your word about the shot coming from outside the store. The bullet was from a handgun, and handguns are pretty innacurate at that range. It's more probable that the shot came from inside the store."

"I didn't say that the shooter was outside the store when the gun was fired. All I can say is that when I looked around, I didn't see anybody either inside or outside the store except Ruth, and she was in plain sight and couldn't have done it. I thought it was most reasonable that the shot came from outside, as I didn't wait a long time before looking around."

"If you knew each other you could have collaborated on killing him," said Wiley. "We'll have to investigate that pos-sibility."

"You won't find anything there," said Ruth. "I assure you we didn't know each other before we entered the store. You won't find any evidence that we knew each other previously. That being the case, each of us is can provide an alibi for the other."

"Lack of evidence to the contrary doesn't prove anything,"

said Ritter. "We'll have to investigate the possibility that you were previously acquainted."

"We'll judge the validity of your alibis," said Wiley.

After a half hour of further questioning, which didn't produce anything new, David and Ruth were permitted to leave.

Once outside, Ruth said, "It's pretty bad. They don't know who kiled Mercer, so now they're trying to pin the blame on us."

"That's the trouble. Until they find the killer, even the innocent are under suspicion."

"I know what we can do," exclaimed Ruth. "We can try to find out who did it, if only for our own protection."

"The problem is," said David. "If the police have no clues, how can we hope to solve the crime?"

"By using our heads. First, we have to find out everything we can about the victim and his friends. The more we know about him, the more likely we are to discover who had a motive for killing him."

"I'm with you," said David. "And we have to learn who among his acquaintances had the skill to hit him between the eyes with a handgun at long range."

"Unless he was shot from inside the store. But we have to be discreet. The police won't like our butting into their territory."

"Have you read the news account of the murder in the local paper?" asked Ruth.

"I should have, but I didn't. I'll look at it today."

"And the obituary should be a further source of information."

"Has an obiturary been published yet in the local paper?"

asked David. "We can also go to the internet."

"I don't normally read the obituaries," said Ruth, "but I'll see if Mercer's obit is in today's paper."

"I'll look too. Great idea."

"Well, so long. See you soon."

Chapter 3

David went home right away to read the newspaper account of the murder. It was on the first page. He learned that Jim Mercer was thirty-two, unmarried, and lived alone in an apartment in town. He turned to the obituary page, but the obit was not yet there.

I wonder whether it will ever appear, David wondered. He cut out the article and put it in a manila folder.

David decided to visit the area where Mercer lived. It wasn't far to Mercer's apartment, and David walked. A few people were staring at the place, and David thought he should question them. He decided not to do so, more from embarrassment than from anything else. It was a silly thing to come here, he thought, and walked back home.

Two days later he saw the obituary in the local paper. He read it carefully and then put it in his folder on the murder.

The obit said tht Mercer was born in Indianapolis and lived there until he went to Indiana University in Bloomington. He studied American history, a fact that went a long way toward accounting for the fact that he was working in a small convenience store. Relevant jobs in history aren't easy to find. According to the obit, the funeral would be held at an Indianapolis church in two days. Mercer's parents both lived in Indianapolis, and he had a sister living in Chicago. Nothing was said about an ex-wife, a girlfriend, or children.

David lost no time calling Ruth.

"Did you see Mercer's obit in this morning's paper?" he asked after the usual hellos.

"Yes, I read it."

"I'm going to go to the funeral in Indy the day after to-morrow. Want to go with me?"

"Of course I'll go with you," said Ruth. "After all, it was my idea to investigate this murder."

"The obituary says that there will be visitation at the church for three hours prior to the funeral," said David. I think we should arrive shortly after the beginning of the visitation time."

"I'm with you on that."

"I'll look up the location of the church on the web," said David. Visitation starts at one P.M. Let's leave right after lunch, say at twelve-thirty."

"I'll be ready. Can you pick me up? Do you know my address?"

"Yes. I heard it when you gave it to the police, and naturally I remember it."

"Naturally," repeated Ruth. Then she added, "My apartment is number four."

"I heard that too. Goodbye now."

On the day of the funeral, David drove up to Ruth's apartment just before twelve-thirty and parked in the street. The location was in a modest neighborhood near campus. It was raining hard. He entered the building and saw that there were eight apartments. Number four was on the second floor. He rang the bell.

"Who is it?" she called through the door.

"It's Dave."

"I recognize the voice. I'll let you in."

David stared at her. She seemed even more beautiful to him than the first time he saw her.

"What are you looking at?"

"You."

"Why?"

"Because you're beautiful. You must know that."

"It's been told to me."

"You must know from looking in the mirror. You don't need anybody to tell you."

"Thank you."

David said, "Are you ready? We don't have any time to spare."

"Ready to go. Do you know how to find the church?"

"I looked up directions on the web. It will be easy. Let's go."

They went down the stairs and into David's car. Neither said anything as he drove away in the rain.

After fifteen minutes, Ruth said, "We ought to have some plans for what we'll do when we get there."

"Yes," he answered.

"I don't think the parents will know anything," said Ruth.

"Maybe not, but we should talk to averyone connected with him."

"What will we say?"

"let's be up front. We were in the store when Jim Mercer was shot. We'll say that we are being treated as suspects by the police, and we want to clear our names. We can do that best by finding clues as to who was the actual killer."

Ruth responded, "The problem with that is that we may talk to the actual murderer, thereby putting our own lives in jeopardy."

"Don't you remember?" said David. "Our names and pictures appeared in the newspaper account of the murder. If the killer read the article, he knows us."

"Maybe he didn't read the paper. If not, he doesn't know our names and faces," said Ruth. Our backs were toward him when he fired the shot."

"It's a chance we have to take if we're going to investigate this thing," said David. "Besides, they know the police are looking into the matter and have a greater chance than we do to find the murderer. What good would it do to kill us?"

"We'll tell everybody we're suspects. Telling the killer will convince him we're a distraction. If he kills us, it will remove the distraction and could provide new clues to the police."

"I doubt that the murderer is as smart as you," said David with a smile.

"I hope not. The smarter we are and the dumber he is, the better our chance of finding him." Ruth also smiled.

It began to rain harder, and David slowed down.

"The paper predicted rain," he said, "but I didn't have any idea it would rain this hard."

"Go slower, please," said Ruth, "or we might not get there at all."

"That wouldn't do us any good." David slowed a bit

more.

They finally arrived at the church's main recreation room a little after one-forty-five. Because of the rain, it took them ten minutes longer than David had expected. About twenty people were milling about, none of whom David or Ruth recognized.

"let's approach people together," said David. A murderer will have more trouble with two than with one."

"I think it best if only one of us approaches each person," said Ruth. "That way we can cover more people in a limited amount of time. We can say we have a companion so if we talk to the murderer, he or she will know we are not alone."

"The killer already knows that there were two of us in the store. He also probably knows our names and faces from the account in the paper."

"But he doesn't know that both of us are investigating the murder," said Ruth. "Let's tell him that."

"There's a problem," said David. "As I said, our backs were to the killer, so unless he read the paper, he won't know us until we start talking to him."

"I've heard that killers always read the newspaper to find out what is known about their crimes. If so, he knows what we look like. Anyway, if we don't talk to him, we'll never know who he is."

"All right. let's split up and begin now," said David. "But let's each notice whom the other talks to so that we don't question the same person twice."

"I'll talk to women, and you talk to men. That way we'll automatically avoid overlap."

Ruth walked over to a tearful woman who was standing

near the casket.

"Are you Jim's mother, by any chance?" Ruth asked.

"Yes, and who are you?"

"I happened to be in the store when Jim was shot. Would you mind my asking you a few questions?"

"What do you want to know?"

"The police are treating me and a man who was also in the store at the time as suspects. We thought that the best way to clear our names would be to discover who shot Jim. Can you help in any way?"

"Do the police know what you're doing?"

"No. We thought it best to keep our investigation confidential, at least until we get some clue. Then, of course, we'll go to the police."

"I'm not sure I should cooperate with you," said Jim's mother.

"You must want to find your son's murderer," said Ruth.. "We can't do any harm, and we might be able to help."

"On the contrary, I think you can do lots of harm. You might alert the person who killed Jim, or you might get killed yourself. I think you're best off staying out of it."

"Thanks for your opinion, but, whether you help us or not, we're not going to stay out of it. But I promise you we'll be discreet and careful."

"All right. I'll help you if I can. What's your name?"

Ruth told her.

"Now what do you want to know?"

"Who were Jim's friends?," Ruth asked. "In particular, did he have any girlfriends?"

"You're not suggesting that his girlfriend killed him?"

"No, of course not. But his girlfriend might have an idea about whether he had any enemies or any serious arguments with anyone."

"He has a girlfriend who lives in Bloomington."

"Do you know her name, address, and phone number?"

"I know her name. It's Sicily Wilmington. She's here now. I'll introduce you."

Jim's mother walked over to a young woman, Ruth following.

"Sicily Wilmington, Ruth Andrews."

"Anders," Ruth corrected.

"Who are you?" Sicily asked with some beligerency. "Are you a friend of Jim's?"

"Sorry, I'm not. I was just in the store in Bloomington when Jim was shot. The police look at me and a man who was also in the store as suspects, and we're trying to clear our names."

"Why should the police suspect you?"

"Because they don't have any other suspects," said Ruth in a matter-of-fact way without really knowing.

Sicily paused a minute, thinking. Then she said, "I'll help anyone who wants to get to the bottom of this. What would you like to know?"

"First, I'd like to know more about you. Where do you live in Bloomington? What is your phone number? What is your email address?"

Ruth took a small notebook out of her purse and recorded the information that Sicily gave her.

"I hope you won't mind if have to call on you at your home in the next few days," said Ruth.

"Not at all."

"Do you have a list of all the people whom Jim knew?"

"I can make a list of those I can think of, but it will take a while. I'll let you know the day after tomorrow. I'll send you an email if you give me your address.

"While you're at it, I'd like to know what their relationships were to Jim and whether Jim was on good terms with them. If there were any arguments lately, I'd like to know that too."

"I'll tell you what I know."

Chapter 4

David saw a man walk over to Jim Mercer's mother and say, "Whom were you talking to?"

"A girl named Ruth Andrews who was in the store when Jim was shot. She has some idea that she can find out who killed him."

"I sure hope so. Why is she interested?"

"She said that the police look at her as a suspect."

"Maybe she did it."

"I don't think so. She seemed genuinely interested in clearing her name."

She sure looks good, thought the man. She doesn't look like someone who would kill Jim.

He left her, and shortly afterward David approached him. "Excuse me, sir. Do you happen to be Jim's father?"

"I don't know you."

"My name is David Stein. I was in the store when Jim was killed. So was a woman named Ruth Anders. She recently spoke to your wife. We called the police to report the crime, and for some reason unknown to us, they regard us as suspects. We're trying to clear our names."

"And you think you can do so by finding the actual killer?"

"We can give it a try. Will you help us?"

"Jim was a good boy. He didn't deserve this. I'll help any way I can."

"Thank you. Did Jim have any enemies?"

"None that I know of. He had a girlfriend, Sicily Wilmington, and, as far as I know, they were on good terms."

"Well, we know Jim was killed for a reason," observed David. "It was obviously not a good reason, but the murderer thought it was. Perhaps it was envy. Do you know of anyone who liked Sicily?"

"I'm sorry. We live in Indianapolis, and Jim lived in Bloomington. When he visited us, he didn't talk much about his life in Bloomington. We...we should have shown more interest in what he was doing, but we didn't want to butt into his affairs. As it turned out, that was a big mistake."

"Don't be so hard on yourself," said David. "You had no reason to think that Jim's life was in any danger."

"You can say that again. How wrong we were."

"What about acquaintances of Jim?" asked David.

"I would think that many of them are here now. Go speak to some of them."

"Can you introduce me?"

"Sorry, I don't know them myself."

"Thank you," said David. He realized he had learned nothing by talking to Jim's father except that he did not know much about his son.

David approached a young man standing by himself. "Hi. My name is David Stein. Would you mind if I took a few minutes to talk to you?"

"Yes, I would mind. I don't know you and I have no

interest in meeting you."

"Please. I was in the store when Jim Mercer was shot. The police suspect that I was the killer."

"The police must have had a reason to suspect you."

"Only that they have no other suspects."

"That's too bad for you." The young man walked away.

This is not going to be easy, thought David. What a disagreeable guy. I'll have to find a way to learn about him, but nothing comes to mind.

David went to talk to another young man. "Hello. I'm David Stein. I was in the store when Jim Mercer was shot. Mind if I talk with you for a little while?"

"Of course not. My name is Sam deAngelo. What specifically would you like to talk to me about?"

"Unfortunately, the police look at me as a suspect in Jim Mercer's killing. As I said, I was in the store when he was shot. The police have no reason to think me anything but an innocent bystander, but since they have no idea who killed Jim, they latched onto me."

"That *is* tough," said Sam. "How can I help?"

"Maybe you know of someone who had a grudge against Jim or who argued with him for some reason. I'm trying to clear my name by pointing a finger at somebody who might have had a motive for murdering Jim."

"Good luck. I can think of several people who didn't like Jim. He wasn't very likeable, in my opinion."

"How did you know him?"

"I know his girlfriend Sicily. I think she was trying to break up with him, and he was resisting. He may have been making things hard for her."

"Do you know why she was trying to leave him?"

"She told me only that she was tired of him but that he didn't want to let her go."

"Who were the other people who didn't like Jim?" David asked.

"For one, the guy you just talked to before coming to see me."

"He didn't even give me his name. Do you know his name?"

"Yes, it's Mike Michaelson."

"Do you know how he knew Jim?"

"No, but I know they weren't getting along."

"What was the trouble?"

"Sorry, but I have no idea."

David said thank you and left to see Ruth.

He pointed to Mike Michaelson. "See that man over there?"

"Yes," said Ruth.

"He wouldn't give me the time of day. Maybe you'll have better success with him. Use the old charm."

"I'll see what I can do."

She walked directly over to him. "Hello."

"Hi," he said. "You're something! What can I do for you?"

"I'm Ruth. Glad to meet you."

"And I'm Mike Michaelson. This funeral seems to be a great place to meet people. How about meeting me for dinner this evening."

"Whoa, not so fast."

"You're the one who approached me. What did you have in mind?"

"I'd like to talk to you about Jim Mercer."

"He's dead, but we're alive, baby. Let's talk about us."

"Sorry, I'd like to discuss Mercer first. Then we can talk about us."

"Anything you want."

"Thank you. Do you have any idea who shot him?"

"I didn't. That's for sure."

"I wouldn't accuse you. I'm just interested in why he was killed."

"All I know is that he wasn't getting on too well with his girlfriend Sicily." He pointed. "She's over there."

"I've met her already, but she wasn't very helpful."

"What makes you think I'd be helpful?"

"Somebody said that you knew Jim well."

"Matter of fact, I did know him pretty well."

"Do you know what the trouble was between him and Sicily?"

"I think she got tired of him, but he didn't know enough to let go. But I'm not sure of that. Ask her."

"Thanks very much. You've been very helpful."

"Wait a minute. You're not going to drop me right away, are you? We're just getting acquainted. You haven't answered me about dinner yet."

"You want a quick answer?"

"Yes."

"No."

"Hey, wait a minute."

"I'm grateful for your help, but I don't need another relationship at the moment. Thank you and goodbye."

Chapter 5

David and Ruth gatherered all the information that they could by talking to people before the funeral. Then they decided to stay for the funeral itself to see what information they could glean from it.

"Jim Mercer was a fine, upstanding young man who died before his time," began the clergyman. "The person who shot him did a dastardly deed. Let's hope the killer meets justice, and soon. I feel for Mercer's parents and for his girlfriend. They must be suffering now and will continue to suffer for a long time."

The clergyman continued, telling where and when Jim Mercer was born (Indianapolis), where he went to college (Bloomington) and what he studied (American history), how he came to live semipermanently in Bloomington, and where and when he met his present girlfriend, but nothing that seemed likely to shed light on why he was murdered.

When David and Ruth left the church the rain was only a drizzle. On their way home the two amateur sleuths talked over what they had learned and what good any of it was. They concluded that they would have to wait for the information from Mercer's girlfriend Sicily, which they expected to receive by email.

David asked Ruth about what she had learned, and wrote it all down. After depositing Ruth at her apartment, he went home and wrote down everything he had learned at the church. He put all his notes in his folder on the murder.

The email arrived two days later. Seemingly the best lead was that Jim Mercer had belonged to a small gun club in Bloomington. About thirty people belonged. They met once a week where the members fired pistols and rifles at targets. Sicily gave them the times and place of the meetings.

A member of the gun club was most likely the killer, David and Ruth decided. they all would know Mercer, and many of the members would be good shots.

"Let's visit them," said David.

"Perhaps we'd do better if we tried to join," said Ruth.

"I don't have a gun, and I've never fired one."

"Neither have I. It's no problem. We're talking about interest, not skill. We can say our interest was awakened when we were in the store when Jim Mercer was shot."

"Should we get guns before we go there?" asked David.

"I think so. It ought to be pretty easy to get a gun. We'll get pistols, as it was a handgun that killed Jim.."

"Good. That way we'll be among people who fire handguns and who also knew Jim Mercer."

"Now is as good a time as any to get our weapons," said Ruth.

They were soon at a gun store.

"Hi," said David. "We're each interested in buying a pistol. What do we have to do to get licensed to carry one?"

"No problem. Come to this counter, and we'll show you what we have."

"We'd like to have something fairly high quality, but not too expensive," said Ruth.

"I have just what you need," said the salesman, pulling out two pistols."

"We'd rather have two different models," said David, "so that we can tell them apart."

The salesman put one pistol back and fetched out another. "These two are similar in quality, and they are easily distinguished. This one is $400 and this other is $425."

"We'll take them," said Ruth. "Dave, will you please take the more expensive one, as I don't have that much money."

"Sure."

"Please fill out these forms, and I can do an instant background check," said the clerk. It took only a short time for David and Ruth to fill out the forms and return them to the clerk. He took the forms and called a number on the phone. After a few minutes he said, "You've passed the background checks. You may take the guns home in their boxes. I suppose you want bullets. They're $20 for 50 bullets."

"We don't just want to keep the guns at home," said David. "We want to be able to carry them."

"You have to make an online application to the state police and pay a fee of $75. Then you have to go to a private vendor for fingerprinting and there is a small fee for that. Here's the address of the vendor. The salesman handed them each the name and address of the private vendor. "Then you go to the city police for a personal protection permit, and there is a fee for that as well."

They both took out their credit cards and paid.

"It's easier than it sounds," said the salesman. "Nothing is hard about owning a gun unless you're a felon."

"I assure you, we're not felons," said David.

"I know that already from the background checks," smiled the clerk.

Several days later they were fully licensed to carry their guns in Bloomington and the rest of Indiana.

"Now to the gun club," said Ruth.

"Sicily already gave us their address and hours. We'll find their location on the web," added David.

It was easily done, and the next day they were at the shooting range. The weather was dry and warm.

"So you want to join our club?" said one of the members who seemed to know what he was doing. "Why?"

David answered, "We were in the store when one of your members, Jim Mercer, was murdered. We were shocked at first, but after a while we thought we ought to have some protection."

"A lot of good owning a gun did for Mercer, but I hope you two will be luckier."

"Neither of us knows anything about firing a gun, so we thought we could learn here," said Ruth.

"We want to learn in as safe a way as possible," said David.

Sicily Wilmington was nearby and walked over to them. "I beilieve that they're telling the truth."

The man talking to them said, "You'll have to show us that you're licensed to carry your guns. Our dues are cheap: ten bucks a month payable monthly or annually. You get one month free when paying annually."

"We'll start out paying monthly," said David. "Here are our licenses and here are twenty dollars for the two of us."

"Thanks," said Ruth. "Here's a ten."

"Thanks," said David,

"This is all costing a lot more than I expected," said Ruth. "I'm beginning to regret that I suggested this."

"Well, now that we've paid for the guns, it won't cost much more," said David.

The man opened a book and entered their names and fees paid.

"I can show them how to shoot," said Sicily. "We shoot only at targets here. What you shoot at elsewhere is your own business," she added, and then with a pause, said, "So long as it's legal."

"When can we start?" asked Ruth.

"What about now?" said David. "Do you have the time now?"

"It happens that I have a few minutes. Come with me to the shooting range."

The three went and found several people there shooting at targets with handguns and rifles.

Sicily walked up to a young man. "Hi Bill, this is David Stein and Ruth Anders, who would like to learn how to fire a handgun. This is Bill Henderson. I don't have much time now, and I would appreciate it if you had the time to teach them."

"I'd be glad to," said Bill. "Why do you want to learn?"

"We were in the convenience store where Jim Mercer was shot and decided we could use some self protection," said

David. "So we went out and bought handguns."

Henderson said, "Mercer had a handgun and was a good shot. Much good it did him."

Ruth ignored his comment. "But a gun is useless unless you know how to use it," she said.

"And that's where I come in," said Bill. "I'll be glad to take the time to show you the basics, but to be a good shot, you have to practice, practice."

"Thanks for your help," said David. "All we want from you are the fundamentals. We'll take care of the practice ourselves."

Bill Henderson spent almost a half hour at the target range with David and Ruth. While they were at it, the conversation ran as follows:

Bill: "It must have been shocking to see Jim Mercer gunned down while you were in the store with him."

David: "What's worse, we didn't have the presence of mind to turn around right away to see who shot him. The one who did it must have counted on us looking first to the victim."

Bill: "You're lucky you didn't turn around right away. If you did, you might now be among the dead."

Ruth: "Jim died instantly, shot between the eyes."

Bill: "The guy who did it must have entered the store, because it would have been fantastic to be so accurate from a long distance."

David: "Jim was a member of this gun club."

Bill: "That's right. How do you know that?"

David: "Sicily told us."

Ruth: "I'll get right to the point. Do you know of anybody

here who was on bad terms with him?"

Bill: "No I don't. Hey Andy, can you come over here, please."

Andy: "What's up?"

Bill: "Do you know of anyone who had it in for Jim Mercer?"

Andy: "Who wants to know?"

Bill: "This is David and Ruth. I just met them. Andy McAllister. He's been a member of the club longer than I have."

Andy: "Why do you want to know?"

David: "I'll be frank with you. The police look at us among the suspects because we were in the store when Jim was shot. We'd like to clear our names."

Andy: "Sorry, I already told the police everything I know, and I don't think I owe you people anything."

Ruth: "Please help us."

Andy: "You're doing only harm by interfering. Just let the police do their job."

Further questions to Andy by David and Ruth got them nowhere, and they soon stopped asking.

After a half hour of practising, they became tired from the strain, and left after thanking Bill.

Chapter 6

"We'll go back next week," said David, "and speak to others. Eventually, I hope we can talk to all of them. It's our best bet to learn something."

"I don't think anyone is going to tell us who did it," said Ruth. "Probably nobody but the killer knows."

"But if there was a significant quarrel between Jim Mercer and a member of the club," somebody ought to know about it."

"That's not proof of anything," said Ruth.

"You're right, of course, but finding a plausible suspect is the first step."

"I don't know that I have enough time to pursue this much further."

"It was your idea in the first place," said David. "You can't quit now."

"I can quit whenever I want to. I can't let this ruin my studies."

"It may hurt your studies a little, but it won't ruin them," David ventured, "unless you spend too much time on it. If you quit, I'll continue without you. But I'd much rather have you with me. Two heads are better than one, especially when one of them is yours."

"Thanks," said Ruth. "Well, I'll spend a little longer on it, but it looks like a full-time job. I can't afford that."

"I can't afford that either."

Ruth smiled. "My original idea was stupid. I had no notion of what we were getting into."

"But it would be great to find the killer."

"If we don't get killed ourselves," Ruth added.

"Let's visit the gun club for a few hours once a week," said David. "That won't take too much of our time. We can cut out movies, and we'll save more time than we lose."

"What! Cut out movies? Are you crazy?"

"Finding a killer is more exciting than the movies. You'll see. We won't even want to go to the movies."

"Especially because of the danger in what we're doing. I'm not sure I like this kind of excitement."

"You will. You'll get caught up in it."

"I'll see you next week, then." said Ruth.

"Not until next week? That's too long. I'm getting to like you."

"Sorry I can't say the same about you. You're too pushy."

"I'm encouraged that you're sorry. Let's meet for lunch tomorrow."

"Next week at the gun club."

The week passed quickly. David and Ruth worked hard at their studies and tried not to think about the murder. In this effort they were aided by the fact that the police did not question them during this time.

When they next met at the gun club, David said,

"Looks like the detectives have given up on us. I knew they would. There's no real evidence linking us to the crime. We didn't even know Mercer in advance."

"I wonder what they're doing now?" said Ruth. I've seen nothing in the paper."

They didn't have to wonder long. The two detectives were at the gun club and approached them.

"What are you doing here?" asked Bruce Ritter.

"We joined the club a week ago," said David. "Anything wrong with that?"

"Strange that you chose to join at this time," observed Ritter. "Why now?"

"The shooting aroused our interest in handguns," David replied. "Ruth and I each bought a pistol and came here to learn to shoot."

"Jim Mercer was a member of the club. It didn't help him, and it won't help you if someone is out to get you."

"Let's hope nobody is out to get us," said Ruth.

"If you keep sticking your noses where they don't belong," said Ritter, "you might prompt somebody to get you both."

Marge Wiley added, "Just because we haven't questioned you lately doesn't mean that you're off our suspect list."

"If we killed Mercer," said Ruth, "then we're in no danger of being killed ourselves."

"You won't find any link between Jim Mercer and us," said David, ignoring Ruth's remark. "We didn't even know him. We just happened to be shopping in the store where he was a clerk when somebody killed him. I really hope you find who did it and why."

"We'll find out sooner or later," said Ritter.

"Better sooner than later," said Ruth. "Then we'll all breathe easier."

"It's far too soon for you to breathe easily," replied Ritter.

"I hope you don't feel as if you have to catch somebody, even if it's the wrong person," said David.

"We don't do that," answered Ritter.

"Well, don't start now."

"Ritter ignored the remark and said, "Come down to the police station with your guns. We want to check them to see if either of them was the gun that killed Mercer."

"But we only bought the guns after Mercer was shot," said David. "Here, I have my receipt with me."

Ritter looked at the receipt. "It seems in order," he said, "but just to make sure, we'd like to examine your guns. Bring them in."

Chapter 7

The detectives left, and David and Ruth consulted.

David: "I suggest that I interview men and you interview women. That way our discussions won't be complicated by extraneous issues."

Ruth: "You forget gays and lesbians."

David: "There can't be that many. My suggestion isn't air tight but can you think of anything better?"

Ruth: "Not at the moment, but you'll have the bigger job. There are more men than women here. I'll start now."

She walked up to a woman who was target practising.

"Hi. I'm Ruth. Dave and I recently joined this club and want to meet some of those already here. Dave is that man in the gray jacket," she said.

"I'm Sara Long and pleased to meet you. I already know you from your picture in the paper. You were in that store buying stuff when Jim Mercer was shot."

"That's right," said Ruth.

"Unlucky you. You're connected with murder, and I guess you and that man in the store with you won't be off the hook until the real killer is found. Unless you're the real killers."

"We're not."

"That's the answer you'd give even if you were," said Sara, managing a smile. "But I'm not accusing you."

"And we're not accusing you," answered Ruth.

"That's good. You have no reason to accuse me."

"My guess is that it was someone from the gun club," said Ruth. "All of you here knew Jim, and all of you know how to shoot. Somebody here had a grudge against Jim. Do you know of anyone like that?"

"I barely knew Jim, and I don't know who his friends were." Sara paused, then added, "Except for Sicily, his fiancee."

"What do you know about Sicily?" asked Ruth.

"Nothing, except that she didn't seem too broken up after Jim was killed."

"Maybe she kept her sorrow to herself," said Ruth.

"I don't know how she felt, only how she acted."

"I learned that there are only about thirty people in this club, and only twenty practice with handguns. That's a small group."

"But if any of them is the killer, it's only one. That's a much smaller group. Or, to put it another way, it's hard to find one among twenty. And if you do find him, he might kill you two as well. Once a person kills, subsquent killings become easier, or so I've heard."

"Him or her," said Ruth. "I sure hope our lives are not in danger. Back to the subject: Could it be that the killer practices with a rifle only, but still used a handgun for the murder?"

"I don't think so," said Sara. "It takes a lot of continued practice with a handgun to be accurate."

"Well, we'll start with the handgun users here, and if that search doesn't find anything, we'll move on to the rifle users."

"Good luck."

David walked up to a nearby man who was sitting down, posssibly resting after target practice.

"Hi. I'm David Stein, a new member of this club, and I'm trying to meet the old members."

"Hi. My name is Ollie Frank. "I know who you are from your picture on TV. You're the guy who was in the store when Jim Mercer was shot. What made you suddenly join the club?"

"To be honest, we're trying to clear our names by finding the real killer."

"A woman was also in the store."

"Yes, Ruth Anders. That's her in the blue sweater," he said. "She's talking to another woman."

"I recognize her too."

"Maybe you can tell me if Jim Mercer had any enemies or if he had a serious quarrel with somebody in this club."

"I'm sorry," said Frank. "I hardly knew Jim and I know nothing about his enemies. I do know that he had a girlfriend who is also a member of this club."

"What's her name?" asked David, although he knew.

"Her first name is Sicily. I don't know her last name. That's her over there," he said, pointing.

"Thanks much. Maybe you can help me by introducing me to some of the other members."

"Sure. Come with me."

David followed Frank to where an older man was sitting.

"Hi, Milton," said Frank. "This is David Stein, Milton Rattinger, our oldest gun-club member."

"Hi, David. I'm not only the oldest member of the club but longest with it. I founded it."

"Pleased to meet you," said David. "You may be the longest member, but I'm the newest. I joined very recently."

"May I ask why?"

"Sure. I happened to be in the store shopping when Jim Mercer was shot. I called the police, but they seem to regard me as a suspect. I'm trying to clear my name. Mercer was shot with a handgun."

"That lets me out," said Rattinger. "I only have a rifle. I use it for hunting and target practice. I'm a pretty good shot, if I say so myself."

"If you founded the club, I guess you know all the members," said David.

"Every one. We're not that many."

"Then maybe you wouldn't mind introducing me to those who use handguns."

"I hope you don't suspect that one of us shot Jim Mercer."

"Well, I understand he was a member of the club, and I guess that he was shot by somebody who knew him. But of course I don't know positively that he was killed by one of you. I just don't know anywhere else to look."

"You remind me of the drunk who was searching for his lost keys at night underneath a lamppost. A policeman approached and asked what he was looking for. He said for his keys. The policeman asked where he dropped them. The drunk said it was across the street. Then why are you looking here? asked the policeman. Because it's light over here, said the drunk."

"I hope it's not like that," said David.

"And I hope it is, but I'll help you if I can. What would you like to know?"

"Who among you had a quarrel with Jim Mercer? Or who had a serious disagreement with him about something important? Was anybody after his girlfriend Sicily?"

"Everybody likes Sicily including myself. She's beautiful and very friendly to everybody. But I don't know of anybody who was 'after' her."

"Perhaps I had better talk to Sicily herself."

"That seems like a good idea. Just remember not to look for keys to this mystery under the lamppost."

Chapter 8

David looked around for Sicily, but didn't see her. He called Ruth and told her that he wanted to interview Sicily again to find out whether anyone was trying to take her away from Jim Mercer.

"She's not here now," said Ruth. "I looked for her a few minutes ago but couldn't find her."

"I'll call her at home," said David.

He preceeded to do so.

"Hello," Sicily answered.

"Hi, Sicily. This is David Stein. I'd like to meet with you some time soon. When are you next going to a meeting of the gun club?"

"Not for a while. Why don't you come over to my place?"

"Fine. When and where?"

"Now is as good a time as any," said Sicily. She gave David the address of her apartment.

"I'll be over in fifteen minutes."

David was as good as his word. Sicily opened the door after he rang once.

"Hello, David. Good to see you."

"Likewise."

"So, what's up?"

"I'll be right to the point. Is anybody trying to make out with you these days?"

She smiled. "People are always trying to make out with me."

"Do you think that one of them could have killed Jim Sherman?"

"How would I know? I wouldn't go out with anyone if I thought he killed Jim."

"How old are you, Sicily?"

"Twenty-two. And you?"

"Twenty-five."

"You're just the right age"

She leaned over and kissed him on the lips.

"Jim was killed pretty recently. Isn't it a little too early for that."

"I liked Jim, but he's gone, and I'm still here. Moping won't do me any good."

"I'm sorry," said David. "I like you but if we become an item, the person who killed Jim might kill me. I'd rather live without you than die because of some jealous person. I hope you understand."

"You don't know why Jim was killed."

"That's just it. I don't know. I'd like to find out but not if it means risking being killed myself."

"Just enquiring about who killed Jim is a risk."

"There are risks and risks. Some I'm willing to try but others not."

"Not even for me?"

"Sorry."

David spent a little more time with Sicily without finding out anything of interest. Reluctantly he left. As soon as he got outside, a uniformed police officer went up to him.

"Will you please come with me to police headquarters?"

"Sure, but why?"

"Because I'm asking you to."

Seeing he would not learn anything until he arrived at headquarters, David reluctantly stepped into the waiting police car. They were soon there.

The police officer took David up to Bruce Ritter's office. "Hi, David," he said. "Sit down, please."

"Why am I here?" asked David.

"Because you were seen going into Sicily's apartment and seen going out again."

"What is wrong with that?"

"It gives you a motive for killing Jim Mercer, that's what. We suspected you from the beginning, but we lacked a motive. Now we have one."

"I was just trying to find out if anybody had a reason to kill Jim."

"Now why would you want to find out that? It's a job for the police."

"I was trying to clear myself against your accusations. But I shouldn't have to be cleared because you don't have any evidence to link me to the crime. You're just fishing."

"We know you were on the scene when Mercer was shot and now we know you have a motive. You visited Sicily to make love to her. All we need now is your confession."

"You'll never get that because I didn't kill him. I didn't make love to Sicily. I don't love her at all. And about Mercer,

I didn't even know him but was in the store just to buy something. Anyway, Ruth Anders was in the store and can give me an alibi. If I'm involved with Sicily, Ruth would have no reason to protect me."

"What did you want to buy?"

"Just a paperback to read. Of course I didn't get it."

"If you confess, it will go easier with you."

"I see you don't have any suspects so you're trying to pin the murder on somebody, anybody. I'm innocent, so you won't be able to tie me to the murder. You'd be much better off if you looked for evidence that would lead you to the real killer. Now I'd like to go."

"I'm sure you would, but stay a while longer."

"You can't hold me."

"Can't I? I'd like to ask you some more questions while you're here."

"I've told you all I know. I'll go now."

"I'd like you to stay."

"I had better call a lawyer."

"All right, you may go now. But we'll get you sooner or later."

"Goodbye."

David went out without looking back.

Chapter 9

When David next met Ruth, he said, "It was a mistake for me to visit Sicily in her home. The police were watching outside and took me in to the police station after I came out. That detective Bruce thinks I went there to make love to Sicily and that she was the reason I killed Mercer."

"I think you had better get a lawyer."

"I think you're right. Do you know of anybody or should I pick one at random?"

"Neither. Ask around the math department. Somebody there should know of a good lawyer."

"It makes sense. I'll do it today."

The following day David went to the math department and asked various faculty members about a good defense lawyer. A few recommended Sean Connery, and David called him up. He briefly told his problem, and Connery asked him to visit him in his office in two days. A woman in the front office told him to enter a rear office.

"Hello, Mr. Connery," said David. "I'm a graduate student in math, and need a lawyer. Three faculty members in the math department recommended you as good, sympathetic, and not too expensive."

"What is your problem?" asked Connery.

"I was one of two people in a convenience store on Kirkwood Avenue when the clerk there got shot. The police stupidly suspect me of killing him, and the other person in the store suggested that I get a lawyer to get the police off my back."

"Why do the police suspect you?"

"I suppose because they have no other suspects. It doesn't make sense. I called 911 on my cell phone and waited for the police to arrive. Why would I do that if I had killed him?"

"What was his name?"

"Jim Mercer."

"I read about the case. Do the police have any other reason to suspect you?"

"The woman in the store with me suggested I get a lawyer. We decided to try to find the killer, since the police have no other suspects. I visited Mercer's girl friend to try to get some information about who might have wanted to kill Mercer. The police were watching her home and decided that I visited her to sleep with her, and that was my motive."

"What is the name of Jim Mercer's girl friend?"

"Sicily Wilmington."

"And what is the name of the girl who was with you in the store?"

"Ruth Anders, an undergraduate."

"Did you know her before?"

"No."

"Then you and she can provide alibis for each other."

"I would think so, but the police think that we are some-how cooperating."

Connery said, "I don't think you have anything to worry about, but I'll represent you if needed."

"Thank you. But before I accept, please tell me what you charge."

"See the girl in the front office, and she will arrange a contract for you to sign. I'll charge only for time I actually work."

David walked into the front office, and received a standard contract, which he signed. The rate was $200 per hour, in increments of a half hour.

"It's not cheap," thought David, "but worth it if it turns out that I actually need help. Let's hope I don't."

When David next met Ruth, she asked, "Did you get a lawyer?"

"Yes."

"Ready to go to the gun club?"

"I hate the gun club, but I don't know any other way to find who killed Jim Mercer."

"I don't have much hope for the gun club, but I don't know what else to do."

They were at the club in fifteen minutes. Another fifteen minutes and they were at the handgun shooting range.

"I'm getting pretty good at this," said Ruth.

"I think you are too, but I'm not."

"You have to squeeze the trigger, not pull at it."

David next told her that he had obtained Sean Connery as his lawyer.

"He charges $200 an hour, but won't charge anything unless I need him."

"Let's hope you don't."

"Exactly my hope," said David.

"Now about shooting your gun," said Ruth.

"I'm trying, I'm trying," Said David.

A stranger walked up to David. "I can help you."

"You can? That's good. "I'm David Stein and this is Ruth Anders."

"Josh Wilmington. Do you know Sicily?"

"Yes," said David and Ruth together.

"I'm Sicily's brother."

"Pleased to meet you," said David. "Do you know any reason why anybody would want to kill Sicily's boyfriend, Jim Mercer?"

"Yes. I don't think Jim was treating Sicily right. In fact, I think he was abusing her. I'm sorry Jim's dead, but I think Sicily is better off without him."

"That's a strong statement," said Ruth. "Don't you think that Sicily might be a better judge than you about her relationship with Jim?"

"I don't understand," said Josh, "why some people stay in abusive relationships against their own interests."

"How can you be so sure about the nature of Jim's relationship with Sicily?," asked David.

"I'm very sure. There were lots of signs of it."

"I hope you didn't act to protect Sicily from Jim," Ruth ventured.

"I wouldn't hurt anybody myself, but I warned Sicily not to permit Jim to treat her the way he did."

"Do you know of anybody who liked your sister and who might have resented the way Jim acted with her?"

"Sorry, I don't, and I wouldn't tell you if I did."

Why not? David thought, but said only, "I guess I'll have to find out for myself."

"You do that and then tell me."

I'll tell the police, David thought, but said "Good meeting you."

When David next saw Ruth, they discussed where they were in the hunt for the person who murdered Jim Mercer.

"Can you believe Josh Wilmington?" asked Ruth.

"He seemed sincere enough, so I tend to believe him. The question is how that knowledge helps us."

"I think we have to look for someone who is interested in Sicily," said Ruth.

"I think so too, but whoever he is, he's not showing himself yet."

"Or herself."

Chapter 10

A week passed without David or Ruth learning anything relevant to the shooting. They met for lunch at a restaurant west of campus in order to size up the situation.

"We've gotten nowhere. I'm for giving up," said Ruth. "We'll remain under suspicion, but the police don't have anything on us, so they can't touch us."

"But they can harrass us," David replied. "I'm for continuing a while longer. Sooner or later, the person involved with Sicily is going to show himself. He shot Mercer for a reason, and if he stays away from Sicily, he will have murdered for nothing."

"Maybe Sicily's brother is right, and the person has no romantic interest in her."

"You mean ke killed a man for an abstract interest in 'justice'?"

"That's unlikely," admitted Ruth.

"So stay with me. We'll get to the bottom of this yet."

"Well, at least I'll pause for a week before I go back to this case," said Ruth.

"I need you to help me," said David. "You have some of the best ideas. Together we can do much more than I can alone."

"I'm taking a week's vacation, and then I'll be back."

"Will I see you during the week?"

"Not likely."

"Then I'll miss you. Take care."

David decided to go by himself to the next meeting at the gun club. While there he saw Sicily talking to a young woman he had not seen previously. He walked over to them.

"Hi Sicily. Who's your friend?"

"This is Sara Long, David Stein."

"Hi Sara," said David. "I haven't seen you before."

"I've been here, and I've seen you. I've also already met your partner, Ruth Anders. "

"She's not my partner," said David, "except in helping me find out who killed Jim Mercer."

"Why would you want to do that? You're not the police."

"We were both in the store when Jim Mercer was shot, and we're trying to clear our names."

"By finding the real killer?"

"Yes. How long have you been a member of the gun club?" David asked.

"Since its beginning, eight years ago."

"Do you use a rifle or a hand gun?"

"I'm equally at home with both. I like to shoot."

"How long have you known Sicily?"

"She's been here about two years. We've been friends a little more than a year."

"Did you know Jim Mercer?"

"Yes, I knew him. I wonder who killed him. The police don't seem to have made any progress."

"I think it was a member of the gun club," said David. "They knew both him and Sicily, and they all know how to shoot."

"You might just be right," said Sara.

"Do you know if he had any enemies?"

"None that I know of," said Sara, "but it seemed to me as if he and Sicily weren't getting along too well recently."

"What makes you think so?"

"It's just that I felt he wasn't treating her the way she deserved. He was brusque at times."

Sicily volunteered, "He didn't treat me like he should have recently, but he didn't deserve to die for that reason. He must have been killed for some other reason."

"Then why?" asked David.

Sicily shrugged. "I don't know why."

"Ruth and I hope to find out," said David. "But it won't be easy. We don't have any clues."

"Good luck," said Sara.

Then she and Sicily went off together arm in arm.

Chapter 11

David was convinced that Sicily did not deeply regret her loss
of Jim Mercer's companionship. He guessed that she was a
woman who lived for the present and didn't dwell on the past.
He wondered why she left arm in arm with Sara. Was it just
what girls do with friends, or was there a deeper meaning?
He knew that Sicily had kissed him and reflected that maybe
she was bisexual.

When he next met Ruth, he suggested that she ask to
visit Sicily.

"Why?"

"I don't dare visit her because of the police. I'd like to
learn whether Jim Mercer abused her, and, if so, whether he
had a good reason." He added, "If any reason can be a good
reason."

"I can do that," said Ruth.

She called up Sicily on her cell phone. Luckily, Sicily was
in and not too busy to see Ruth.

"I'm in luck," Ruth said. "She's willing to see me now."

"It's too soon to say you're in luck," said David. "After
the interview we'll see how lucky you are. So I'll wish you
good luck."

Ruth said goodbye and walked over to Sicily's apartment.

"Come in," said Sicily after Ruth rang the bell.

"Hi Sicily. Thank you for letting you see me on such short notice."

"Thanks for coming. Are you here to see me or to find out something?"

"Both."

"Let's get business out of the way first, and then you can see me for pleasure."

"I'll get right to the point," said Ruth. "I met your brother, and he tolod me that Jim Mercer was abusing you. Is there any truth to that?"

"Yes, for some weeks. I was getting tired of him and made remarks about leaving him. He couldn't take that and tried to keep me with him. It got to the point where I actually became afraid to leave him."

"That's ironic," said Ruth. "You were afraid, but he was the one to be killed."

"No matter how badly he treated me, he didn't deserve that. I'm genuinely sorry for him, although his being gone simplified things for me."

"Did anyone else try to make love to you after he was gone?"

"Actually, I tried to make love to David, but he wasn't interested. I wonder why not. Are you and he lovers?"

"You've been frank with me," answered Ruth. "I'll be equally frank with you. No, we are not lovers," at least, not yet, she thought.

"What's the matter with you?" said Sicily. "Do you have somebody else?"

"Not at the moment."

"Don't you want a lover?"

"I'll want the right man, I suppose," Ruth replied. "I'm not convinced that David is the right man."

"You certainly are particular."

"May we get back to the original subject? Do you have any other lovers now?"

"I think that's a question I don't wish to answer. Sorry."

"I hope you're not trying to protect anybody."

"I can tell you that I wouldn't want as a lover anyone who would kill Jim Mercer or anybody else," said Sicily. "It's not true that all's fair in love and war. Kiling a rival is going way too far."

Ruth felt that Sicily was sincere in her objection to anyone who would kill for her. But did anyone do so? Sicily did not give any clues to who might be a rival for her affections.

"Are you finished quizzing me yet?"

"I guess so," said Ruth.

"Then let's get to the social part of things. Would you like a cup of coffee?"

"No thank you."

"A glass of wine, then?"

"I believe I will, thank you."

"Red or white?"

"You choose. I'll have what you have."

Sicily went to her fridge and pulled out an opened bottle of white wine. The cork had been put back half way. She took two glasses from her cupboard, each of which she filled.

"To your health," said Ruth.

"To us," said Sicily.

"To us?"

"Yes, to you and me."

"It seems like a strange toast, but I'll drink to it," said Ruth.

They both drank their wine.

Sicily than approached Ruth and kissed her on the lips.

"Wait a minute," said Ruth. "What are you doing?"

"I like you and I'm showing that I do."

"I like you too, but not in a kissing way."

"If you like me," said Sicily, "don't be shy about showing me."

"I'll invite you to dinner at my house. How about Thursday at seven?"

"You move slowly," said Sicily, but it's a step in the right direction. I had something more immediate and more intimate in mind, but I accept dinner."

"Thanks for the wine. Goodbye now," said Ruth and left.

Ruth called up David as soon as she left the apartment.

"Hi David, I just left Sicily's place after finding out something important about her."

"What?'

"I think she's bisexual."

"What gave you that idea?"

"She tried to proposition me."

"She has the right idea. I'd like to proposition you myself."

"No, thank you."

"Did you accept her offer?"

"Not exactly. I invited her to dinner at my place."

"That's practically an acceptance. Are you crazy?"

"I hope not, but I'm not sure. Everybody's a little crazy, I suppose."

"Please, don't sleep with Sicily. She seems like a promiscuous woman, and you wouldn't be safe."

"I hope I know how to take care of myself."

"Perhaps with a man, yes, but do you have any experience with a woman?"

"Not yet."

Chapter 12

On Thursday promptly at seven Sicily rang Ruth's doorbell. Ruth let her in and Sicily promptly kissed her.

"I invited you to dinner, nothing else," said Ruth rather coldly.

"Why would you do that unless you wanted it to be followed by something better?"

"I don't know. Let's concentrate on dinner. It's almost ready. Have a seat."

"You're really a beautiful woman," said Sicily. "I haven't met anyone as beautiful as you. You attract me."

"You're certainly not shy," replied Ruth.

"Why should I be shy? I've never achieved what I was after by being shy."

"Look, Sicily. I'm heterosexual."

"I think you've no experience yet with any woman. How do you know what you are?"

"You don't know what my experience has been. Please do me the respect of believing me when I say I'm straight."

"You won't know for sure until you try."

"That's for sure. But I invited you to dinner, not to my bedroom. So let's sit down and enjoy dinner. Afterward we

can discuss anything else we want to talk about."

They sat down and had a simple meal of mushrooms, broccoli, cod, salad, and strawberries, together with bread and wine.

"I appreciate the good meal. Thank you," said Sicily. "You're not only beautiful but you can cook."

"Thank you, especially for saying that I'm beautiful."

"You mmust know you are. A woman always knows what she looks like. There are mirrors in every home."

Ruth said, "I've never met anybody as determined as you. No wonder Bruce Mercer was jealous."

"I admit I wasn't faithful to him, but he didn't have to treat me so bad after he found out. But none of this has anything to do with you and me."

"I agree with you there."

"Good. Now lead me to your bedroom, and we'll see what happens."

Ruth took her hand and together they walked to Ruth's bedroom.

They emerged from the bedroom one hour later.

"How did that feel?" asked Sicily.

"I have to tell you that it felt good, but it doesn't mean that I'm going to make a practice of it."

"Yes, you will."

Ruth didn't answer.

"I'll go now," said Sicily. "See you soon."

The next time Ruth and David met, he said, "Well, what did you find out?"

"Nothing except that Sicily and I are both bisexual."

"My God!"

"It's an important clue."

"I didn't think you could be so reckless. You saw what happened to Jim Mercer. The same thing could happen to you. Please end this now, for your own safety if for nothing else."

"To tell you the truth, I got caught up in things and didn't think about my safety. But I had better start thinking about it now, if it's not already too late. I'm really not the reckless type."

"Well," said David, "maybe not ordinarily, but you sure were thoughtless with Sicily. She's not in danger, I hope, but you are."

"I'll have to stop seeing Sicily. Period."

"And I have already made up my mind not to see her, except to talk to her casually. In the future we'll have to get our clues from talking to other people. But I still think our best bet is the gun club."

"I'm even afraid of going to the gun club," said Ruth. "Too many guns scare me."

"Somebody has to have a reason to kill you. If you stop seeing Sicily, except to say hello, I think you'll be all right."

"You think, but you don't know."

"We can only go by the probabilities," said David.

Ruth said, "I'll be safest by staying away from the gun club for a while."

"You have nothing to lose by skipping a week."

"I'll do that, but it might be more than a week."

"You're usually careful, but you have to be careful all the time. Usually is not enough. But you don't have to be fearful.

As I said, I think you don't need to skip going to the gun club. Just don't get chummy with Sicily, and you'll be safe."

"Maybe it's already too late."

"I don't think so. The person who killed Jim Mercer didn't act until things were bad for some time."

"OK, you've convinced me. I'll skip next week and then go back the week after. And I'll be cool to Sicily."

David went alone to the gun club the following week. He spent a half hour practising without getting much better. "Ruth is much better than I am at this," he thought. "But I still believe that practice will get me better, if slowly."

Sicily dropped over. "Hi, David. Where's your friend Ruth?"

"She decided to stay home this week. I hope she'll return next week."

"I hope *you* will see me, though. What about after dinner tonight?"

"I like you, Sicily, but in view of what happened to Jim Mercer, I think it's safest to stay away from you. I hope you'll understand."

"Jim Mercer wouldn't let me go after I wanted to go. I think that's why he was killed. You'd let me go if I wanted to leave you, so there's no problem."

"I'm sorry, but I don't know why Mercer was killed, and until we catch the killer, I'm not going to get involved with you."

Besides, he thought, I'm in love with Ruth. I guess I'm not somebody who can be in love with more than one person at one time. So far, Ruth is not reciprocating, but I hope she will. I'm going to be optimistic and keep trying, but not so hard as to scare her off.

Chapter 13

The next time David and Ruth met, she opened the conversation with

"I don't think we're making any progress. Finding Mercer's killer is a tough nut to crack."

"On the contrary," said David. "I think we've made lots of progress. We've discovered that Sicily is bisexual, or, rather, you've found it out."

"But that only widens the possibilities for the murderer. Now we know the killer could be either a man or a woman. How does that help us?"

"The more we know, the more we're helped," said David. "You're being too pessimistic."

"But what do we do next?"

"I admit I'm not sure," said David. "I suggest we see what Sicily does. My guess is that the person she goes out with the most is the likely killer."

"But she seems eager to go out with anybody who will have her."

"Well, neither of us is likely to go out with her again."

"Some help that is!" said Ruth. "We already know that we didn't do it."

"Patience," said David. "I feel that continued observation of Sicily will tell us who did it."

"I hope you're right."

The next morning, David received a telephone call at home. He picked up.

"Hi, this is Bruce Ritter. I'd like you to come to the police station this morning."

"Sorry," said David. "I now have a lawyer, and I have to find out when he's available. I won't go without him."

"We can pull you in."

"Fine, but I won't say a word without him."

"All right. Call your lawyer and come at his first available opportunity. Let us know in advance so I'll be sure to be here."

As soon as David hung up he called his lawyer.

"Sean Connery's office," said the secretary.

"This is David Stein. I'd like to speak to Mr. Connery."

"He's busy right now, but I'll tell him. If you give me your number, he'll call back as soon as possible."

"Today?"

"Today."

David gave his phone number. and decided he'd have to stay at home waiting for the return call.

In the afternoon Sean Connery called him. "What's up?"

"David Stein here. The police want to see me as soon as possible. I said I would only speak if accompanied by my lawyer, and you're him."

"I can go with you tomorrow afternoon at three, if that's all right."

"I think so. I'll have to check with the police."

David checked and found the time acceptable. He called his lawyer, and the secretary said that Connery would meet him at the police station.

David appeared at Bruce Ritter's office promptly at three. Ritter was there but not Connery.

"Let's get started," said Ritter. "Have a chair."

"I'll sit down, but I won't say anything until my lawyer arrives."

"Suit yourself. I'll be back in ten minutes."

Connery arrived five minutes late.

"I'm glad you could come," said David.

"So am I. I'm a very busy man." Connery sat down in a chair next to David. "I'm glad there's nobody with you now. As I understand it, you spoke with the police earlier."

"Yes, I told them what happened. I had no reason to hide anything, and I didn't dream that they would treat me as a suspect."

"Then I'm afraid you can't keep silent now. I'll prevent your answering any leading questions, but I can't do any more than that for you."

A few minutes later Ritter entered the room. David stood up and introduced his lawyer, who also stood up.

"We know each other," said Ritter.

"Hello," answered Connery and offered his hand.

The two men shook, and then all three sat down.

"You would be smart to confess," said Ritter. "Then it will go easier with you." He paused, "by far."

"I object," said Connery. "My client has nothing to confess."

"I've told you all I know," responded David. "It's the whole truth. There is nothing more to say."

"Say it again."

David looked at Connery. "Do I have to say it again?"

"I'm afraid you do. Once you've talked, you have no right to keep silent."

David went through the talk once again, in almost the same words as previously, as he knew them by heart.

Connery spoke up. "What my client says is quite reasonable. How many times are you going to ask him to say it?"

"Over and over again until he confesses," said Ritter.

"You're harrassing him," said Connery. "You may ask him reasonable questions, but not over and over again. I protest." Connery spoke to David, "You don't have to reply to the same questions repeated endlessly. You may say that you've already answered the questions more than once."

"OK," said David. "May I go now?"

"Yes, you may," said Ritter. "But we'll get you one way or another. It will go easier on you if you confess now."

David and Connery both left without saying another word to the police.

Once outside, David asked, "How can I stop them from wasting my time by calling me in again and again?"

"You can't without my aid. "I'll petition a judge to stop the police from harrassing you. If that works, then you'll be free of them unless they find new evidence. If the judge doesn't agree, I'll think of something else, but I won't worry about that now."

"New evidence?" cried David. "There isn't even any old evidence."

"I'm inclined to believe you," replied Connery.

"Thank you. Goodbye," said David.

"Goodbye," said Connery, and they parted.

Chapter 14

When David next saw Ruth, he told her that the police called him in again and that he had to call his lawyer to avoid being harrassed.

"You poor dear," said Ruth.

"I'll be OK," David replied. "Connery will take care of it."

"Connery?"

"Have you forgotten? He's my lawyer."

"Oh. That's right. Stupid of me to have forgotten."

"Ruth, I've told you before that I'm very fond of you."

"That's good."

"Don't you like me at all?"

"Of course I like you. If we never saw each other again, I'd miss you."

"I love you."

"I'm flattered, but I don't love you."

"I hope you will get to love me."

"Why should I?"

"Because I'm young, smart, and love you."

"Those are good reasons but not sufficient."

"What would be a sufficient reason?"

"Time. Give me enough time, and I might get to love you. Of course, I can't guarantee anything."

"You are just the woman I want."

"Thank you. You're very kind."

"Thank you. That's also a reason to love me."

"I said to give me time, and we'll see what happens."

"Fair enough. You haven't ruled it out."

"That's right. Be encouraged."

"Let me kiss you."

"On the cheek."

"Better than nothing." He kissed her. "Delicious."

"I'll go now," she said, and she went.

David was encouraged by the conversation. He decided that it was just a matter of time before Ruth would respond to him in a way he thought proper. The first thing they had to do was to find who killed Jim Mercer, but they weren't making good progress. The longer the wait, the more stale would be the scent.

But there was nothing he could think of doing until the next meeting of the gun club, and that was almost a week away. He decided to concentrate on his schoolwork during the next few days, Unfortunately, his mind kept wandering back to the murder. This will never do, he thought. I need a vacation. But where?

He decided on Fort Lauderdale, even though he couldn't easily afford it. He went on the web and examined a ticket for a five-day stay. He found a a flight with hotel on the beach for a discounted price and took it, paying with his credit card. Two of the days were Saturday and Sunday, so he would miss only three school days. He left the following day, and would be back in time for the meeting of the gun club if all went well.

Arriving in Fort Lauderdale, he called the hotel and got a free ride in their car. He had chosen wisely; the hotel was full of young people. Shortly after arriving, he sat down to dinner at a table with three girls and two boys. After introducing himself, he said that he was going to be here only five days so that he had to make friends in a hurry.

He spoke particularly to the girl without a partner and asked her, "What's your name, When did you arrive, and how long are you staying?"

"I'm Esther Morgan. I came three days ago and will stay another four. Glad to meet you. It's about time I met a handsome guy who is interested."

"I'm very interested. Lucky for me. My name is David Stein."

After dinner David and Esther left the others and went for a walk on the beach.

"This is a good hotel," said David. "I picked it by chance because they had a discounted rate."

"Glad you did," said Esther. "I also got a discounted rate combined with the air fare."

"Where are you from?"

"New York. I'm attending NYU."

"What brings you here at this time?"

"We have a spring break. And you?"

"I'm going to Indiana University grad school in Bloomington. We already had our break, but I'm taking a few days off because I feel the need for a change. Two of the days are on a weekend, so I'm only missing three days of school."

"What are you studying," asked Esther.

"Math, and you?"

"I'm majoring in French. In August I'll take a year off in Paris and really learn the language."

"Are you all set up already?"

"Yes, I'll be staying with a French family. They have a daughter going to NYU this year, and I met her in one of my classes."

"Good break for you. You'll be speaking French without an accent."

"I wish, but it doesn't work like that. You have to be under twelve to learn a language without an accent. But if all goes well, I'll be speaking fluently with only a slight accent."

After walking twenty minutes, they took another twenty to walk back to the hotel. It was not yet dark.

"Let me show you my room," said David. "Unfortuately, it doesn't have an ocean view. Those cost more."

"But the view won't be necessary for what we're going to do there," said Esther, smiling.

Chapter 15

David returned to Bloomington on schedule more than satisfied with the way his Fort Lauderdale vacation turned out. He immediately called Ruth.

"Hello, this is David. Did you miss me?"

"Oh, have you been gone?"

"Yes, I was away for five days. Didn't you notice?"

"You didn't call. That was a blessing."

Anything new happen while I was gone?"

"No. I suppose I should ask you where you were? Where were you?"

"I took a small vacation in Fort Lauderdale. While there I met a girl named Esther from New York."

"New York is far away. You won't be seeing her very often."

"I'd rather spend the time with you. Let's have dinner this evening."

"Where?"

"In a Chinese restaurant, Third and Jordan. I'll meet you there, say at seven?"

"I'll go, just so we can plan how to pursue our quest for Jim Sherman's killer."

At the restaurant, after the usual "Hi's," they ordered. Then Ruth said, "I'm sorry, but I haven't been thinking about the case."

"What have you been doing, then?"

"Going to classes and studying."

"Have you learned anything interesting?"

"No. I learned a lot but it wasn't interesting."

"Maybe you're in the wrong field."

"I don't think so. Very little I've learned in school is interesting. It's the things I learn outside of school that are interesting."

"What have you learned outside of school?"

"Wouldn't you like to know!"

"Yes, I would."

"One thing I can tell you that you already know. Just by going shopping you can become a suspect in murder case."

"It's very unlikely. My guess is that it will never happen again."

"I sure hope not!" exclaimed Ruth with fervor.

"Well, now is the time to go back to Jim Mercer. Can you think of a new strategy?"

"Let's see whom Sicily spends most of her time with," replied Ruth. "That's the one who is most likely the killer."

"At least it isn't one of us," said David. "How will we keep track of her?"

"One way is to go regularly to the gun club."

"That's fine, as far as it goes," said David, "but we'll have to watch outside her apartment as well. Otherwise we'll be at this business too long."

"Let's begin tomorrow evening," said Ruth.

"Why wait until tomorrow?"

"Because I'm busy tonight."

David went home to make up for lost work. Shortly afterward, he received a phone call. He picked up.

"Hi, this is Esther Morgan. Is that you David?"

"Yes, it's me. What's up?"

"I enjoyed meeting you in Fort Lauderdale and wondered whether we could keep a good thing going."

"Where are you calling from?"

"New York."

"It's too far away. I'm too busy to travel to New York once a week to see you."

"I can visit you."

"Yes, you can, but I'm very busy. I'm a grad student in math, as I've told you, and I have to work hard to keep up. I'm already behind in my work because of the time I spent in Fort Lauderdale."

"But I gathered from your seeing me in Fort Laud that you thought the trip was well worth it."

"Look, Esther, it wouldn't work out."

"Don't jump to conclusions. Let's see."

"Please, I know what I'm talking about. I just don't have the time."

"You mean you don't want to see me. People always have time for what they want to do."

"Please, Esther, we had a good time, but it's over. Go on to something else."

"You took advantage of me," said Esther.

"I didn't think so. But whether I did or I didn't, we're done. You should find friends in New York."

"You'll regret dumping me."

David said, "Goodbye, Esther," and hung up.

Ruth and David immediately put their new strategy to work of watching Sicily, writing down the name of everybody who was seen with her. They also wrote down the date and time of each meeting. If they didn't know the person, they asked around until they found out. Unfortunately, the number of people on the list was half a dozen, but after another week, those at the top of the list were only three: Andy McAllister, Bill Henderson, and Sara Long.

"I'll bet it's Andy, Bill, or Sara," said David.

"You're probably right," agreed Ruth. "Which one?"

"Andy is by far the most disagreeable one," said David, "so I'll vote for Bill or Sara."

"That sweet girl?" remarked Ruth. "How can you believe it?"

"It's because she's so sweet that I think she has something to hide."

"For the moment, let's assume you're wrong," said Ruth. "Let's watch Andy carefully. If it doesn't work out, we'll switch to Sara?"

"How can we tell whether it is working out?"

"Let's watch all three of them at the gun range," suggested Ruth. "Let's see who is the best shot."

"Great idea."

At the next meeting of the gun club, it happened that Andy, Bill, and Sara were all at the firing range. Andy and bill were reasonable with their handguns, but Sara was a crack shot, hitting the bull's eye with regularity.

"Sara's our man, or rather our woman," said Ruth. Do you think she is using the same gun she used on Mercer?"

Let's ask the police to examine Sara's handgun," replied David. "Suppose she killed Mercer. What, then, would she do with the gun? If she got rid of it, she'd have to buy another, and that very fact would go a long way to incriminate her. I'm guessing that she kept her gun, not thinking that the police would want to examine it."

"That's a good idea, but suppose the police don't agree?"

"Let's wait until everybody is gone, and then we'll dig a bullet out of the target. We'll hand it to the police and hope that it has the same markings as the bullet that felled Mercer."

"How will we know which bullet to take?" asked Ruth.

"Simple. We take a bullet from the bull's eye. Sara was the only one who hit it."

At their earliest possibility, they dug out the bullet.

"Ruth, take this bullet to the police and ask them to compare it with the markings on the bullet that hit Mercer. Tell them that we got the bullet from a gun Sara Long shot at the target. Then tell them to examine Sara's gun."

"What if the bullet doesn't have the same markings?"

"I'm confident it will," said David. "Sara shot Mercer, and all the police have to do is examine her gun to prove it."

"What if they refuse to look?"

"You ask them. If they say no, tell them that they have fixated on us so much that they won't look anywhere else. Shame them into it."

"All right," said Ruth. "I'll do it. No time like the

present."

"I suggest you go over to the police station to make your point with Ritter," said David. "That's better than just phoning him."

Chapter 16

At the police station Ruth asked to see Bruce Ritter. After a twenty-minute wait, she was shown into his office.

"What do *you* want?" said Ritter. "We'll pick you up after we get the evidence on you."

"I'm here to show you evidence that somebody else shot Mercer."

"How can you do that?"

"I have here a spent bullet from the gun that shot him. It belongs to a member of the gun club, Sara Long."

"We'll examine the bullet, but how will we know whose gun it came from?"

"If the marks on the bullet are right, get a search warrant and ask for Sara Long's gun. I believe you'll find that her gun was the one that was used."

"We have no evidence that Long shot Mercer. You're only trying to divert evidence from yourself."

"Give it a try. You haven't been able to find any evidence that either David or I did it. Maybe you'll have better luck with Sara. The bullet will give you enough to get a search warrant."

"How do we know that the bullet came from Sara's gun?"

"We saw her shoot at target practice at the gun club.
After they all left, we dug the bullet out of the target."

"If Sara Long shot Mercer, she would have ditched the
gun somewhere."

"And bought another? That would only call attention to
herself. I admit that I can't prove that Sara shot him, but
that's what the police are for. Examine Sara's gun and go
from there."

"What makes you think that Sara did it?"

"She was going out with Sicily, and we suspected she was
jealous. Also, we saw her at the gun club target practice and
she was very accurate. We fished the bullet from the bull's
eye."

"We'll first look at the bullet, and if it matches, we'll
decide what to do next."

Bruce Ritter's men examined the bullet and found that it
matched. Then they obtained a search warrant and obtained
Sara Long's gun. They took it to the lab and found that it
was the gun that was used to kill Jim Mercer.

"Well," said Bruce to Marge. "We have the proof. Sara
Long is the killer."

"I never suspected her," said Marge.

"Neither did I. We had no reason to suspect her."

"How did Ruth Anders come to suspect Sara?"

"By seeing how she behaved with Sicily."

They went to Sara Long's apartment and told her that
her gun was the one used to shoot Jim Mercer.

Surprised, Long confessed to the shooting.

"He was abusing my friend," she said with tears in her
eyes.

"That's no excuse for killing him," said Ritter. "I arrest you for the murder of James Mercer. Come with me, please."

"Well," said Ruth, "we finally caught the killer, thanks to our persistence and to a lucky break."

"Let's celebrate," said David. "Come to my apartment tomorrow for dinner."

"I'd like that. What time?"

"How about six-thirty?"

"That suits me fine. I'll be there. Thanks much."

"Is there anything you don't eat?"

"I'm omniverous."

The following day Ruth rang the bell five minutes after the appointed time. David let her in.

"Hi, Ruth. Dinner is just about ready."

"Good. I'm hungry. And here is a bottle of wine. It's red, a Bordeaux of medium price but I hope of good quality."

The meal consisted of mushrooms, chicken breast, asparagus, and sweet potatoes, with bread and wine, then a tossed salad, and blueberries for dessert.

"Thank you," said Ruth. "It was a delicious meal."

"You're welcome."

"And now what?"

"I love you, Ruth."

"That's good. I love you too."

"That's the best news I've heard in a long time. I've loved you almost at first sight."

"Almost?"

"Well, maybe it was at first sight. Then I knew only that you were beautiful. Now that I know you better my love is much deeper."

"I didn't love you at first sight," said Ruth. "I thought you were too pushy."

"But you love me now."

"Yes."

"When did you start loving me?"

"Not for a while. Maybe it was love at tenth sight."

"If you love me, let's make love."

"Yes. Yes. Yes."

Don Light is the pen name of a professor emeritus of physics at Indiana University. He retired after thirty years of service. Since his retirement, he has written seven novels, including the present one. His previous novels have the titles, *The Runners*, *The Physics of Murder*, *The Deep Green Society*, *The Red Chestnut Bookstore*, *Murder in Academe*, and *Occupying Bloomington*, all of which are available from AuthorHouse.com or from Amazon.com.